CW00868512
Isabella's
Birthday
Party
with
Thunder
HF Beaumont

To order additional copies of this book, contact:
Xlibris
1-888-795-4274
www.Xlibris.com
Orders@Xlibris.com

ISBN: Softcover 978-1-7960-8620-1
EBook 978-1-7960-8621-8

Print information available on the last page

Rev. date: 02/11/2020

Grandma, grandpa, mom, dad and little brother Aidan, Isabella, went to see the Lake Elinore Storm, A-Advanced baseball team play one evening. They have a mascot Thunder, similar to a comical dog, he's green wears a baseball hat and jersey, does some amazing things to get the fans wound up. Cheering him on, he performs between innings.

We all thought that Isabella would be afraid of Thunder. She surprised us all when she ran towards him and gave him a hug. She was very young five years old, and small in height, Thunder got on his knee and gave her a huge hug, that was all she needed from him, he was her favorite reason to attend the baseball game. She only wants to watch him, baseball was boring, to her.

Isabella was a cheerleader for the local Pop Warner Football team, she would sit on a five-gallon bucket with all the rest of the cheerleaders when the team did not have the football. They performed for the parents during the timeouts and half time.

She was very good at shaking the pom-poms, really got into the whole idea of performing in front of the parents. As her grandpa it was so heart warming to see her with such joy and enthusiasm. Grandma always bought donuts and hot chocolate for her and coffee for her parents, every game a parent was assigned to bring the girls snacks, finger foods, chips and candy.

Her birthday was fast approaching, mom asked Isabella, what do you want for your birthday? I want a party; can I invite Thunder? Please mom, please. It was imperative to get a hold of the team to see if Thunder could come to her party. The parents met Thunder, showed him the photo of Isabella, he remembers her giving him a very loving hug in between the innings of a certain game the team was playing. Isabella's mom was hesitant when she asked him if he could attend her birthday party. Thunder asked, is her name is Isabella, a very cute little girl with a great smile? She even has a twinkle in her eyes. I remember her, thought about her the entire game, looked at all the fans until I found her sitting with her family, said Thunder.

Isabella's mom asked if he would show up for her party, he hugged her mom and said try and stop me from showing up. Of course, I'll be there, give me the address, date and time of the party, I'll be there, count on it. They talked about the price and the deal was complete. They kept it a total surprise from Isabella.

There were so many presents, family members, and neighbors at her party. Her daddy was burning the burgers, hot dogs, and other items on his grill. All the kids were playing, making lots of noise. About an hour after the party started, Isabella's daddy answered the doorbell. Standing there was a young man carrying a duffel bag. When he told her mom and dad who he was, they showed him to the nearest restroom. Then they found Isabella, who was running around with her friends. "Daddy and I have one more surprise for you," Mom told her.

Close your eyes, all of you kids, close your eyes, don't peek, keep them closed until we say open your eyes. They waved Thunder, into the backyard. Ready on the count of three open your eyes, all the parents counted for the kids, one, slight pause, two, another slight pause and three open your eyes. The screams were so loud it rocked, the moon sideways. Isabella ran over to Thunder, and gave him such a big hug, made sure he was introduced to everyone attending the party, this is my grandpa, this is my other grandpa, this is my grandma, so on and so until he shook, all of our hands. She introduced all the kids who were attending her party, to Thunder.

STORM

Then she showed Thunder, her plastic playhouse, which she just got for her birthday. She and Thunder, got inside of the playhouse, through, the front door, how he did that, I will never know. They sat in the playhouse and played.

Tears of joy was streaming down many cheeks during most of the photo shoots. This was a once in a lifetime golden memory. So sad when Thunder, had to leave, he had another birthday party.

Everyone, who had a camera on their cell phones took photos. Isabella got photos, of Thunder, with all the female family members. Holding her in their arms as she was hugging Thunder. He received, a life time of hugs and kisses from my precious granddaughter.

STORM

The two must have hugged for five minutes, tears were running down Isabella' cheeks. She thanked him for coming to her party, mom and dad escorted Thunder, out of site of the kids and Isabella, so he could return to his human form.

He told mom and dad, she is a remarkable little girl, she brought me to tears. I'll never forget this day, thank you for having me, attend her birthday party, gave mom and dad a hug.

CPSIA information can be obtained
at www.ICGtesting.com
Printed in the USA
BVHW020857230220
572989BV00011B/3

* 9 7 8 1 7 9 6 0 8 6 2 0 1 *